RHODA'S ROCK HUNT

For Jasper,
and for Josh and Liz
—MBG

For Owen and Jonah
—JAB

MINNESOTA HISTORICAL SOCIETY PRESS

Text ©2014 by Molly Beth Griffin. Illustrations ©2014 by Jennifer A. Bell. Other materials ©2014 by the Minnesota Historical Society. All rights reserved. No part of this book may be used or reproduced in any manner whatsoever without written permission except in the case of brief quotations embodied in critical articles and reviews. For information, write to the Minnesota Historical Society Press, 345 Kellogg Blvd. W., St. Paul, MN 55102-1906.

www.mhspress.org

The Minnesota Historical Society Press is a member of the Association of American University Presses.

Book design by Colleen Dolphin, Mighty Media

Printed in U.S.A.

10 9 8 7 6 5 4 3 2 1

∞ The paper used in this publication meets the minimum requirements of the American National Standard for Information Sciences—Permanence for Printed Library Materials, ANSI Z39.48-1984.

International Standard Book Number

ISBN: 978-0-87351-950-2 (cloth)

Library of Congress Cataloging-in-Publication Data available upon request.

Molly Beth Griffin was a fiscal year 2012 recipient of an Artist Initiative grant from the Minnesota State Arts Board. This project was originally funded, in part, by the Minnesota State Legislature from the state's arts and cultural heritage fund with money from the vote of the people of Minnesota on November 4, 2008.

RHODA'S ROCK HUNT

MOLLY BETH GRIFFIN   ILLUSTRATIONS BY JENNIFER A. BELL

When Rhoda's Auntie June and Uncle Jonah took her on a long, long hike from their up-north cabin, her shower was a bucket of cold lake water,

her dinner was salami and cheese,
and her bed was a skinny little pad and a ratty sleeping bag.

But she didn't mind...

...because of the ROCKS.

Rhoda loved ROCKS.

Smooth rocks and bumpy rocks and sparkly rocks and stripy rocks
and rocks shaped like hearts and hats and horns.

"All right," Auntie June said,
"but you have to carry them in *your* pack."

They were moving camp every day
and had to carry everything in big, heavy, bulky packs.

Rhoda's pack was smaller, but she was in charge of hauling it through woods, and over streams, and to the Big Lake all by herself.

One day, they hiked through a beautiful birch forest with rustling leaves and birdsongs overhead.

Rhoda found jagged rocks and bumpy rocks in that forest and one with tiny sparkly bits that glinted in the dappled sunlight. *Ooo!*

Into her pack they all went—*Ooof!*—and Rhoda trudged on, wiping sweat off her forehead.

"Looks like someone needs a bucket shower!" Uncle Jonah joked.

Rhoda didn't laugh.

The next day, they crossed a rushing stream
with whispering water all around and dragonflies whizzing past.
Rhoda found lots of smooth, round rocks in that stream
and one with a curve that fit into her palm just right. *Ooo!*

Into her pack they all went—*Yarg!*—
and Rhoda waded on, slumping under the weight, her tummy grumbling.

"Sounds like someone needs more salami!" Auntie June joked.

Rhoda didn't laugh.

That night, Rhoda hardly slept at all.
A pinecone poked her through that skinny little pad,
and her ratty sleeping bag was damp and stinky.

So she was tired and dirty and hungry on the last day of their trip, and crabby, too—

—until they arrived at the Big Lake.

Waves crashed on the shore, and gulls called overhead.
The water stretched out to the horizon,
and the beach was covered with millions and billions of rocks!

Rhoda ran her hands over all of those sun-warmed treasures.

She found red ones and blue ones and stripy ones,
and then she looked harder, and found tiny banded ones
that glowed the color of sunsets. *Ooo!*

Into her pack they all went.

"Time to go," Uncle Jonah called.
"It's not far now!" said Auntie June.
At the end of this one last hike, the cabin!
A real shower, a hot meal, a soft bed.

Rhoda jumped up and grabbed her pack and hoisted.

But nothing happened.

She pulled and pushed and panted—*Ooof! Ooof! Yarg!*—

but the pack
wouldn't
budge.

"Help!" she cried, but her auntie's arms were full, and her uncle was all loaded up.

This pack was Rhoda's to carry,
and it was
full of
ROCKS.

She couldn't leave her treasures.
She tried loading up her pockets,
but the weight made her shorts sag,
and she couldn't hike like that.

She thought about staying on that beach forever,
but Auntie June and Uncle Jonah were waiting.
Besides, Rhoda really needed a shower, and dinner, and bed.

She loved her rocks—all her beautiful **ROCKS**—
but she couldn't keep them all.
She had to let some go.

So she took them out, one at a time,
and stacked them
on a table-like slab down by the water.

Rhoda worked with the weight of each rock,
with the curves and bumps and bulges of each rock,
until *all* those forest rocks and river rocks and Big Lake rocks

Well, almost all.

Back into her pockets went the one glinting forest rock,
and the one palm-snuggling river rock,
and a small handful of tiny glowing agates from the Big Lake.
Then she smiled at her rock cairns,
the towers of souvenirs she was leaving behind.

Finally she slung her pack onto her back
and followed Auntie June and Uncle Jonah
all the way to their cozy cabin
where a hot shower,
and a delicious dinner,
and a soft, soft bed
were waiting
just for Rhoda,

and a sun-warmed windowsill
was waiting
just for her very best **ROCKS**.